The **SATURDAY TRIPLETS** in

The Pumpkin Fair Problem

The **SATURDAY TRIPLETS** in
The Pumpkin Fair Problem

by Katharine Kenah
Illustrated by Tammie Lyon

SCHOLASTIC INC.

For the Deans and Spaldings, with love
—K.K.

For Gus and Do-Do—thanks for the company
—T.L.

ISBN 978-0-545-48144-1

Text copyright © 2013 by Katharine Kenah.
Illustrations copyright © 2013 by Tammie Lyon.
All rights reserved. Published by Scholastic Inc.
SCHOLASTIC and associated logos are trademarks and/or registered trademarks of Scholastic Inc.

12 11 10 9 8 7 6 5 4 3 2 1   13 14 15 16 17 18/0

Printed in the U.S.A.   40
First printing, September 2013
Designed by Jennifer Rinaldi Windau

It was Saturday morning.
The triplets were eating breakfast.

"Let's do something," said Carlos.
"Something fun," said Bella.
"I know," said Ana. "Let's go
to the Pumpkin Fair!"

The fair was full of rides.

They could make scarecrows.
They could eat cookies.
Or paint their faces.
It was hard to choose!

"Let's find a ride that goes
up and down," said Ana.
"No!" said Bella and Carlos.

"Let's ride horses," said Bella.
"No!" said Carlos and Ana.

"Let's listen to music," said Carlos.
"No!" said Ana and Bella.

"Rides are best!" yelled Ana.

"Horses are best!" yelled Bella.
"Music is best!" yelled Carlos.

"Stay together," said Mom and Dad.
"We will," said Ana.
"We will," said Bella.
"Don't worry," said Carlos.

"I see a ride that goes
up and down!" shouted Ana.
She ran toward the ride.

"I see horses!" shouted Bella.
She ran toward the horses.

"Listen!" shouted Carlos.
He ran toward happy music.

Where is Ana?
Where is Bella?
Where is Carlos?

"Here we are!" called the triplets.
"We found horses!" said Bella.
"We found music!" said Carlos.

"We found them on the same ride!"
said Ana.

What a perfect Pumpkin Fair!